Topic: Celebration   **Subtopic:** Seasons

Notes to Parents and Teachers:

It is an exciting time when a child begins to learn to read! Creating a positive, safe environment to practice reading is important to encourage children to love to read.

REMEMBER: PRAISE IS A GREAT MOTIVATOR!

Here are some praise points for beginning readers:

- You matched your finger to each word that you read!
- I like the way you used the picture to help you figure out that word.
- I love spending time with you listening to you read.

Book Ends for the Reader!

Here are some reminders before reading the text:

- Carefully point to each word to match the words you read to the printed words.

- Take a 'picture walk' through the book before reading it to notice details in the illustrations. Use the picture clues to help you figure out words in the story.

- Get your mouth ready to say the beginning sound of a word to help you figure out words in the story.

Words to Know Before You Read

Christmas tree

Easter Bunny

fall

lake

pumpkin pie

spring

summer

winter

A Year of Fun

By Carl Nino

Illustrated by
Chiara Fiorentino

Rourke
Educational Media

rourkeeducationalmedia.com

It is spring.

Easter is here!

We go on an egg hunt.

Hello, Easter Bunny.

It is summer.

We go to camp!

We swim in the lake.

We sing songs.

It is fall.

It is Thanksgiving Day!

We see our family.

We eat turkey and pumpkin pie.

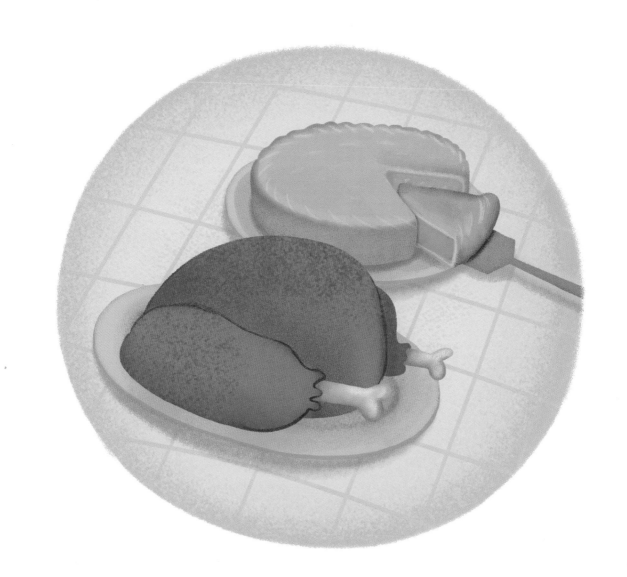

It is winter.

Christmas is here!

We decorate the Christmas tree.

We get presents.

Holidays are fun.

We like all seasons.

Book Ends for the Reader

I know...

1. What season is Easter?

2. What do we do on Easter?

3. What season is Christmas?

I think ...

1. What is your favorite thing to do in summer?

2. What is your favorite thing to do in fall?

3. Which holiday is your favorite?

Book Ends for the Reader

What happened in this book?

Look at each picture and talk about what happened in the story.

About the Author

Carl Nino is an avid reader and loves writing about all kinds of things. He loves to travel and is trying to visit as many countries as he can. He enjoys learning about the different cultures and traditions of people all around the world!

About the Illustrator

Chiara Fiorentino is a children's book illustrator, born in the Italian countryside. She is deeply fascinated by underwater creatures and whimsical animals. When she isn't drawing, she loves taking long walks, doing hand knitting, or taking a break for a chat with her friends.

Library of Congress PCN Data

A Year of Fun / Carl Nino

ISBN 978-1-68342-707-0 (hard cover)(alk.paper)
ISBN 978-1-68342-759-9 (soft cover)
ISBN 978-1-68342-811-4 (e-Book)
Library of Congress Control Number: 2017935353

Rourke Educational Media
Printed in the United States of America, North Mankato, Minnesota

www.rourkeeducationalmedia.com

Edited by: Debra Ankiel
Art direction and layout by: Rhea Magaro-Wallace
Cover and interior Illustrations by: Chiara Fiorentino